Killing
Delilah

Killing Delilah

TRACY RYAN

FREMANTLE ARTS CENTRE PRESS

First published 1994 by
FREMANTLE ARTS CENTRE PRESS
193 South Terrace (PO Box 320), South Fremantle
Western Australia 6162.

Consultant Editor Wendy Jenkins.
Designed by John Douglass.
Production Coordinator Tony George.

Typeset in Times
by Fremantle Arts Centre Press
and printed on 89gsm Husky Bulky
by Lamb Print, East Perth, Western Australia.

National Library of Australia
Cataloguing-in-publication data

Ryan, Tracy, 1964 - .
Killing Delilah.

ISBN 1 86368 068 3.

I. Title.

A821.3

to
Doron Samuell

ACKNOWLEDGEMENTS

Some of the poems in this collection have appeared in *Blast, Fremantle Arts Review, Going Down Swinging, Imago, Island, LINQ, Luna, Mattoid, Naked Eye, Properties of the Poet* (editor P. Kavanagh, 1987), *Salt, Southern Review, Summer Shorts* (editor Peter Holland, Fremantle Arts Centre Press, 1993), *Westerly.*

Some poems were also broadcast on ABC Radio, 100FM, 6UVSFM and 6NR.

The poem sequence 'Streams in the Desert', in an expanded form, shared the Mattara Poetry Prize in 1987.

Publication of this title was assisted by the Commonwealth Government through the Australia Council, its arts funding and advisory body.

Australia Council
for the Arts

Fremantle Arts Centre Press receives financial assistance from the Western Australian Department for the Arts.

CONTENTS

Arrival		11
Ménage à trois		12
Four Poems:	1. Animal	13
	2. Littoral	13
	3. Thaw	14
	4. Fertility	15
In the First Place		16
Hair		17
Letter to the Future from Late Capitalism		18
Guest House, Margaret River		19
Morningswood		20
Prepossession		22
Wise & Foolish Virgin		23
Streams in the Desert:	Taking the Habit	25
	On the Absence of Mirrors	26
	Dove	26
	Cell	27
	Leaving	27
Haworth		28
Bern		29
Liquidambar		30
How to speak frankly		31
Basel Zoo		32
Bison, Perth Museum		33
Mist		34
Le grand Meaulnes		36
Reconciliation		37
Raisa Gorbachev's Cherry Red Dress		38
Serenade		39
Killing Delilah		40
Contraband		41
At Night, After		42
Prickly Pear		43
say we were ...		44

Norfolk Hotel	45
Old Love	46
City Girl	47
Second Thoughts	48
Exorcism	50
Offering	52
The Land of Counterpane	53
Familiar	54
Jagoe Street	56
Anniversary	58
Cuts	59
Reconnaissance	62
Split	64
Things Like This	65
Decree Nisi	66
Tea for Two	68
Bread	69
Pianoforte	71
Ever After	72
The Snow Queen	74
Post-Partum	77
Deadlock	79
& if you said jump in the river I would	81
Imprint	82
Nine South	84
Merna	86
Psych Ward	88
A Visitation	90
O.T.	91
Phone	94

ARRIVAL

When the last dove didn't come back
to the ark, Noah knew
another world was turning

now as my body shuts down
its flows, fresh ground is opened

far more than forty days & nights
you float   recapitulate
each creature in your growth
already wiser than I am

I am
so exclusively human

trusting my judgement
where will you alight?

I can't pledge
safe passage
as God could
if there were God

but I have danced years for these rains
after barrenness

believe in something inside
my flesh & outside

the earth's many faces renewed
words   in love   made good.

MENAGE A TROIS

When Mossy brought death home
after a night out where I thought
she'd been at it on heat,
she dumped her bird like guilt
on the carpet, easily discarded.
Crouched under a sideboard,
she pleaded, wide-eyed,
the conquest's easy, but after?

There was nothing else for it.
Back to the garden
this poor parrot
meant only to visit
and in with it, under a bougainvillea
whose brightness tells lies
without words, though I suppose
to be vegetable's
already no small advantage
in a murderous world:
I too would keep quiet.

Even the ground wasn't about to yield
but it's done now, and that's that.
I don't live here, never planned to get involved.
The tenant was out, and Mossy's her cat.
Now the earth-wound is closed over,
Mossy's shut out with the knowledge
of her buried quarry, and between us
the glass, the silence of a lovers' tiff.

Four Poems

1 Animal

You move into me as a frantic
animal runs for cover
don't look back
over your shoulder

I want to take you in completely
but you are diverse and never
all in one place
you are a whole kingdom

What has been set
between us

Who is the hunter?

2 Littoral

You pull out of me like
an undertow
leaving traces
salt taste on the surface and
my bed's empty
as the seabed
after high tide
at the edges.

Day by day it
overtakes us
knows us
more than we do.

See what we're left with
water distortions
repeated patterns
littoral
refuse dragged
from other places.

Everything washes up here
but again and again we insist on
coming back.

3 THAW

This is the breakthrough, this is the new
age that follows the ice.
My eyes focus for the first
time on you in another light.

How do you look so human when
I thought
you were striding the waste
places   inescapable
in your pursuit?

It wasn't you but
a figment of
the cold
monstrous creation
piece by piece from
others I'd met and
fragmented.

Now the whole world is fluid
I look outside   I love you
reaching you slowly as in water.

4 FERTILITY

My moonbelly waxes and wanes
drawing you with me like the sea

These bodies are not
godlike as we once
thought but only subject
to laws   to cycles
from outside

Our love then is luxury
syncopation
play against meter or
ornament to fact
we celebrate
because we can't
escape

Yet I am glad to be caught here.

In the First Place

In the first place was something other than this.
I know that, though I couldn't tell you
where the first place was.

It was somewhere between the fur and
looking slightly ridiculous
with our sleek skin on

or perhaps even earlier.
I wish, I wish I could remember
the way back there.

The trees, the earth, look familiar.
They call me back to before
we got separated.

I want to lie down beneath them
become what I was in the first place
in the first place where we knew how to

mate and die without talking
of love because
love was obvious

love the first time and the first place.

HAIR

The length
of my body is an odd
nudity, what is it
doing there, how
did the hair
get pared down
to just
these patches
we cultivate
like fetishes
meant to excite
when we want
to play animal
or we control
to stress and make
the difference
between sexes
as if otherwise
we couldn't find
ourselves.
I can't force
what once was
to grow now
in a strange season.
I'm caught
between
the dream of befores
that paralyses
and the need
of my own nakedness
which is there,
which is there.

LETTER TO THE FUTURE FROM LATE CAPITALISM

Now that the ottoman's only
a chair &
a rare one at that
& all we call mogul's the one
who enjoys an
empire of daydream   & debt
I wonder which words will remain when
our powers are spent
& whether you'll bother to trace
your origins in
our impotent bequest
names that in our time could buy out
cities   politicians
people's hearts   almost
unknown in your vocabulary
quaint as some antique
& foreign coinage
without clout or currency
                              – if anything survives
I hope it'll be
the voices we muted
our own & others
telling a time beyond
putting a price on
the words you speak must
be our verdict.

GUEST HOUSE, MARGARET RIVER
for my brother

1

The dining room was once an Anglican cloister.
It takes time
to work this out.
The frame has shifted.
The feeling is gone.
Maybe I sleep in a cell
where soft words fell with all their repercussions
on walls not stone but
fragile as the ears of God
or were never said
both guest and host
finally evicted.

2

This is my second visit
ten years after.
There is no trace of you here.
I checked the visitors' book
but they change it yearly.
Why is it I remember
the food we ate here
the beds we slept in
yet you, your words, remain
so stubbornly gone?
Windows here face inward
pointing to the sky like Mary.
The sun passes through my day
without stopping.
Things keep moving.

MORNINGSWOOD

Playing with fire.
Dad lets me carry in
sticks and twigs for the kitchen
stove. *Morningswood*, he says.
Mum corrects him: *Kindling.*
Well, where I come from, Dad begins,
and it begins again.
I say nothing
never name
this stuff that sets it all alight.
That narrow mouth with its sliding grate
consumes all that's useless, does away
with cover-ups, old news, stale arguments
and in exchange
feeds and warms us. We take it for granted.
Buttering up the jaws
of the old jaffle-iron
we metamorphose
all last night's leftovers
smashed peas that slid round the plate
stiff remnants of potato mash
and hated carrots –
into a crisp toast-pocket that'd
sizzle the roof of your mouth off.
One way to make her eat veges at least –
says Mum – *but it's dangerous.*
Sitting this close to the source
my face is burning.

Later, bringing sticks in again
to fire up my own hearth
I dare the word
Morningswood.
My husband looks up
sees the hard logs give way
flames taking all the unsaid
we make bonfires of.

PREPOSSESSION

Don't want to dress you up   no
coat of many colours to
set you apart   set you up
yet this red possesses me   I knit
into it each breath and movement
my fingers spin an outside
world for you while inside
you spin bone and flesh and blood
your flutter sharper than this red
riding the tides of breath
in your nakedness I plan
already how to cover
once I was clear as you are
but years have layered round me
language   lies   and gender
this red defies the codings
this red is to reveal you
alive and just beginning

WISE & FOOLISH VIRGIN

in brown box pleats above brown smudged knees
kissing Brenden the new boy because
if you didn't he'd drop you
(there was always Branca
back in another
mining town he could return to)
      they even shared the same initials

lunchtimes you spent
sneaking into the church
to check out
the pamphlets
always the same one sought out & toyed with

VOCATION

you had a life to spend
on God or
some other worthy man
calling

now you call
your own tune
imagine
you've left that place for good
& maybe you have
or do you only roll it up like those
partly-worked
altar-cloths stitched
every Friday afternoon
while Sister read from *Coorabeen*
never never done with
      the devil finds work for idle hands

one day maybe you'll
unfurl & start
madly embroidering
some stranger's design waiting
filling in shapes in time for that phantom
groom to return.

STREAMS IN THE DESERT

TAKING THE HABIT

Now no longer to know the name
under which the untapped days
were numbered out; as from a dream
to wake and rise

now across and outside time
to move in him as water flows
you cannot drain or dam the stream
that simply is.

Now no longer to know the claim
of duty, definition – those
are merged in being what I am
one word of his

and I am wearing small and seem
to care no more for her that was
before the flood, before the flame
that never dies.

Now no longer to know the name
that shamed and hid her from his eyes:
act and identity are come
to still waters

ON THE ABSENCE OF MIRRORS

There is no getting around it:
your vanity's mortally wounded.
At first you appeared to miss us
now, stripped to the barest
essential, you're gladly without us.
Don't ask the world around us
to give back your facial features:
it can't leave a true likeness.

Where is she gone, that child
abandoned to the world?
Windows are frosted over
lest the night outside give answer.
Another must replace her.
Cast down your eyes, beware
that last glimpse over shoulder
the odd dark pool of water.

DOVE

Under the refectory window, face down
it waited. Somehow it seemed blasphemous
to go on gardening. It was no use.
Now, I could recall, there had lately been
a sad unsaintly odour round that bed
like the strong tasteless stories we were read
to keep our minds off eating while we ate.
Drawing this grass curtain, articulate
in its dry revelation, hard last word;
delicately weeding around the dead bird
I could not bring myself to bury it.

CELL

It is not walls, it is not
wood it is not
shutters, floor or stiff straw
sack it is not
brick or clay or morning-cool
soul-bracing water from our pitcher
it is not thickened knees
from wax polish and prayers
it is not withered palm, bare crucifix
neither the Virgin vigilant
neither our coarse white night veil
still intact when day breaks;
it is not necessarily in this place
it is not this space of ten square feet
trying its best to be emptiness
(O poverty O joy)
it is ancient and modern
compact and portable
it is this cold hard fact: our cell
is the solitary heart.

LEAVING

like everything else here
is done in silence
the stunned silence of one
coming up after drowning.

There is no way around it.
For the second time I shall become
nothing but memory.

HAWORTH

This is a Victorian evening.
Snow-muffed trees bow and curtsey,
hiding night's passion.
Houses doze on one another's shoulders
or stare at the lost horizon.

At the top of the town
the parsonage is walled-in, empty.
Smoke ghosts from the chimney.
Streetlamps halo shadows: going, gone.
It is illusion.

Only the gravestones are solid.
Windows are barred, but birds have flown
leaving golden eggs,
frost-feathers snagged on glass.
My feet crunch in steps
already printed.

BERN

In the pit they dance.
Eyes miserly and yellow
feign disinterest. It's not for you
we dance, they say,
and in a way that's true.
We live for the odd tossed carrot
the winterwhite dreaming of bearbreath
mingled with small of survival.
Here's five centuries' memorial
to your founding slaughter
but you can only circle
patronizing
watch and marvel
pay your way into the world
of the animal.

LIQUIDAMBAR

Autumn's changeling, a sprightly thing
lithe-limbed, inviting.
Who knows where you lead to?
Mast for a tall ship of dreamery
or tower for tumbling tresses.
I climb you gladly.
Your topmost branches
still touch the same world
I knew in childhood.
Over a sea of blue tiles
I survey your seasons' kingdom.
And now you strew
your shower of stars,
a crunchy red carpet
that winter walks in on.

HOW TO SPEAK FRANKLY

is the first and last
question I'll ever ask
if I press
the trees for straightness
each reply is different
bending its own way
if I look to
the river for clarity
it only gives back
a million little lives
my own image on many surfaces
real depth & apparent depth
I can't tell apart
or interpret the sky
rains in several directions
I must accept this
as the earth   nowhere solid
accepts my equivocation
yields to my tread like everyone else's
takes me
finally
as my own answer.

BASEL ZOO
for Susanne

Winter, walking in,
a kangaroo
two black swans
and in the reptile house, an old bobtail.
I smile
try to tell my friend
but she can only press nose to glass
and wonder,
read facts to me in dialect
I can't catch.
Luege, Mami, luege! a child cries.
Later, in snow outside the zoo
squirrels leap
imaginary walls.
My mouth falls open:
Look!
She smiles.
The hemispheres meet.

BISON, PERTH MUSEUM

Finally plucking up guts enough
after twenty years, to face you
humpback stuff my dreams were made of
shadowing me since the age of five
or perhaps since birth –
I catch you now stopped in your tracks

My mother introduced us
against my will
tried to tell me you weren't alive
but what did I know of preservation

Am I really so much bigger
or are you shrinking

No screams this second time around
Language is mine now, I can read
your Latin name

Ah but you and I know
what that wedgehead drives at
what big teeth you have
when I consent
to let you out.

MIST

shrinks all mornings to your own backyard
and you decide
solitude's not that bad
since you have no say in it
it's as if all your guests
suddenly left the room
and you're alone
with the smoky after-party wreckage
seeing things differently
wondering why you ever asked them
alone is so pure

mist
dilutes the landscape   soap in your eyes
or a bad hangover
you know the trees
the animals
are out there somewhere
but don't care

mist
possesses you   a new vision
you add another layer to keep out
the damp but still
it enters   washes you out
till you are white
and indistinct
and glad of it

mist
fills the nostrils   an oxygen mask
loving you to life
you can push it away but they'll insist
you have no breath to argue   can't
see where you are so
give yourself over
colours would hurt now

mist
grips at your chest   an accuser
tells you: no further
maybe the operation failed and
you've moved on
this is heaven   though you don't know it
cold and senseless
white past any point of return.

LE GRAND MEAULNES

We can never go back there now
The dark has fallen fast
We must press on somehow.

Our lake a stagnant slough
Castle come down to dust
We can never go back there now.

The grass grey-haired, the plough
Grown dull and laid to rest
We must press on somehow.

We live by the sweat of our brow
An angel guards the east
We can never go back there now.

No use asking how
the garden path was lost
We can never go back there now
We must press on somehow.

RECONCILIATION

What the hell is she thinking of?
Two years divorced from a God
she couldn't learn to love
and here she is
crawling back to him.

It's the loneliness that brings it on,
a need to make things right again.
Everyone said it couldn't last.

They meet by proxy
in a dark room like a closet.
He only speaks through stand-ins.
Their conversation is formulaic.

No violence in it, just
mental cruelty
irreconcilable differences.
There's a whole list of them
she'll reel off.

They need this ritual.
It's a secret code
she's to know his henchmen by.
They come down hard on her
but it's better than silence.

Bless me, Father ...

Raisa Gorbachev's
Cherry Red Dress

Raisa wore a red dress
instead of black
to meet His Holiness
or so they call him
in certain quarters.

Some said red for Russia
Some said red for a sister
not in mourning for any man
refusing to darken
the self kept under
that grants all power.

I think Raisa rather
said: Other people's gods
don't need me.
If I don't speak their language
no plea   no order
can move me.
I don't consent
to costume or custom
however well-meant

I wear
what blossoms from inside.

SERENADE

All that tuning's working up to something
bush muffling, bees humming
like primed strings
birds rehearsing solos
in counterpoint.
For them there's no difference
between practice and performance.
They're in love with the process.
Their show's gone on a long time
before we listened
and doubtless will continue.
But how they serenade us just the same!
Struck dumb with incidental music
we accidentals join the song
by adding silence
sink like a perfect cadence
into the night.

KILLING DELILAH

Because I have lived too long with her
and for her, blinding myself
by degrees, calling it love.
My other half, I said.
She became my interpreter.
I relied on her charms to get me through
a foreign land.
Strength was all I had
but she did away with it
quietly, while I slept
a lifetime
till her words spoke for me
and her ways won out.
I thought her face was my own face,
put faith in her social graces –
she was always in demand.
But sooner or later someone
was bound to ask for me.
Now is the moment of release,
my only chance.
My fingers are feeling for the cracks.
One sure blow is all it takes
to bring this house down.

CONTRABAND

After a while you stand steady,
grow sea-legs,
learn to negotiate an ocean of silences.
He's the breath you catch between words,
insinuations in the spaces. This emotion
a cargo you're not sure you want to carry:
there's a high price on it.
How'd you get into this piracy?

There are whole gulfs between the tables
where you sit, where he sits,
gaps you've no right to navigate
above all in public, putting others at risk.
Steer through that archipelago of eyes,
uncharted and potentially enemy.
One slip and you're done for;
nowhere's safe harbour.

AT NIGHT, AFTER

Blind slide of thighs
over now
side by side they lie
each withdrawn
snail horn
frail into the carapace
this skin-stuff masquerades as.
Or thin ice, flimsy glaze
of more than eyes,
mute surface we
subject the world to,
some things come in through.
Nothing stays, though.
Hair hides her face
hands lock
like swords at back of neck
protecting from
his sleeping sound, her sighs.

PRICKLY PEAR

All the time it was growing in my garden
I never knew it could be eaten.
What a source of pleasure I'd ignored.

He introduced it, saying
You could survive on that.
Knocking it off with a stick
delicately he took it to the kitchen
with the quick expert slit of a surgeon
handing me the heart of it on a spoon.

Tastes like kiwi fruit, I said
but that wasn't quite it – those seeds
tart grits, a reminder of something different
sprung from the wilderness, persistent.
Not all things are easily come by.

Later I heard from someone else
of the million near-invisible quills
that can catch on your skin if you're careless.
He hadn't mentioned that.

SAY WE WERE ...

say we were two hemispheres
whole lives apart
yet meeting at edges

you could never leave me
I was your shadow
closest when unseen

in the full-on
noon of tropics
I was the night

say we were two languages
that never quite translate
we were something

nearly meant
every sentence
leaves unsaid

say we were left
right   black   white
cold   heat

love   hate
whatever you like
I am

here at your return
the line
we draw is arbitrary

but permanent:
say you can never leave me
you are not mine.

NORFOLK HOTEL

Part of the pleasure's the mess you leave
for others to clear up.
Under the circumstances it didn't feel wrong
departing from the daytime script.
Conscience is so abstract.
But this room's real, real as a playhouse
after the event.
The lavender drapes are let down now.
On the twin beds you improvised into one
the covers are rumpled, shed selves.
Carpet's christened as you drip
from the quick shower, reborn a stranger.
But something in you is familiar.
In the dark she learned
its lines, memorised his gestures
whoever he was,
his snores, his leaving
the toilet seat up.
You, whoever you are now, dressed
in someone else's husband, wear
these small things like a flower
in your lapel
so she'll know him under your skin.
6:17. You're gone before breakfast.
She combs the room for clues you leave behind.
A dropped dollar coin as if last night
were a wishing well;
a Redback matchbox, empty.
She pockets it.
You leave her
a vague sunrise over Freo, the account
theoretically paid up.

OLD LOVE

like a poem you wrote and then forgot
surprising you years later
with its fine form and feeling.
Too easy to gloss over
the agony, the teasing
that made it hold together;
the hard work, blank rejection,
critical scorn.
All you see now is harmony
swallowed whole, not tasting it.
lines stuck like fishhooks, stubborn
and piquant.

New love yet to be written.

City Girl

had a lover once who
always talked of the Blue
Mountains where
mauve light charms rifts
into gullies and poems
grow in lichen.

They met in town
down the alleys of Northbridge
one hour a week in his offices.
He regretted this tawdriness
unfortunate backdrop
to modern romance
somehow wrote sonnets to the highrise blocks -
all so much raw material.

His words made a way to
another world, pure pastoral
come live with me I'll leave my wife.

Try as she might she still saw
straight streets   slums   department stores
the soon-dead novelty of elsewhere;
herself in an old role
written out   discarded
said no and left
him momentarily at a loss
for metaphor.

Second Thoughts

1 THE SAME

and afterwards   he washes his hands and mouth
to spare his wife, pulls on the same pants and says
got to pick her up at six   sorry
it's five to six   he's a considerate husband
you spit out   *isn't she LUCKY*

2 MESS

but he's in your mouth
like words you know
by heart and can't repeat
the taste is flat
he leaves   the bottom of your world
falls out again like shopping
look at the mess
he's made no you've both made
red wine on the rug
like bad blood
there must be a way to get out

3 CLEAN

she
keeps a clean house
her husband's never home in
except with you when she's out working
those pill-bubbles of her cycle
you saw in her bathroom
are efficiently empty and on time
everything here's discreet
you let your kitchen run riot
don't clean the carpet
can't be bothered anymore with shopping

you timeshare with her
the cost's enormous but
nothing you can't handle
you meet her by absence   the gaps in his voice
he says he'll ring daily

4 DINNER PARTY

at last you meet   he's sure she has
no clue
if only you'd a good word
to stab him with
but he never turns his back
you see her screaming in body
language he can't interpret
you could translate but instead
play dumb
why the hell doesn't
she fight for him
on second thoughts   don't answer

EXORCISM

This house remembers you as I do:
making easy, entering at will
self-styled tenant for a time

Windows were worn at edges, boards bent
before you
entered, I grant

and all already sinking.
Everything seems untouched though vines
grow thicker and tighter now

across the verandah
choking out sunlight
holding together

bougainvillea, old soul
tossing its scarlet
billets doux at my door.

This house, assemblage of desires
endlessly restored,
the stains uniquely yours

indistinguishable now from
anything else,
part of a past again

and again rewritten
to suit,
absorbed by floors like footfall

but not forgotten.
Here at the hearth the same
flames light other faces

so many visitors –
no one stays,
no ghosts but

you, invisible film
on my skin, unshifting
air I move in.

I sprinkle these words like water
to cast out
low spirits.

OFFERING

The man is paper you say and so
I know what must be done
destroy the volatile
old notes   poems   in that sticky
unshiftable spider's hand
photos   mementoes of any kind
his name excised from the flyleaf
of every book   my life   the story
will be ours from now on
                                    I dig a pit
in the hard ground
slit the offending things
into seven pieces   the only magic I know
but it's will that counts
layer it with each leaf of him
whose lies have seeped now
between us as chemical spill
does irreversible
damage   ignite   the images peel
back and squirm
blackened to lace
shadows of themselves
pages that played
messenger in regrettable
hotels   fall limp
sharp in the nostrils but
I force myself to feel
it   this is not torture
I stand over but
my first offering
there'll be no more victim
the fire spits
toward its end under my bucket
staticky as radio   contact cut
I mean to see this through.

THE LAND OF COUNTERPANE

You sleep easily beside me now
and these quilted hills are dumb
not even the surface
swells and hollows show
what moved   like a tremor
beneath this cover
opening new gullies
your kittens tumble into   knowing
no difference between bodies
ready to call us home
treading our love like water
we shift and shift again but
don't ever have to leave here
we can change the face of the earth like this
overnight.

FAMILIAR

I'm glad I didn't
know you then

rats & I have
nothing in common

think of disease
London plagues
part of a dim &
dingy past

You say
He was intelligent
we called him Kitty
he used to run
all over me
perch on my shoulder

you grow wistful at
pet shop windows
pleading his cause but
I insist

over my dead body

and over my head
at night they run
his rowdy brothers
shut up in the attic

sometimes the noise
dwindles
our cat   vigilant
picks them off
one by one
we suppose
though they must be
big as he is
judging size
by this new silence

scuttling in the brain
long after all are gone

I sleep with one arm
round our baby daughter
dream they issue
forth from walls
like secrets that
couldn't be held
any longer

you laugh & say
domestic rats
are different.

JAGOE STREET

Daily they come back like bullies
to finish the job –
five men & machines against
one cottage
across the road
a carcass picked over nightly
by locals, themselves on notice.

It's not the first & won't be the last –
other yards sit dumb with pain,
gaps in a row of teeth
whose decay, unsightly,
demands removal.

We chose with eyes wide open
this street under siege,
hoping the house's eventual fate's
not meant as metaphor
for our unsure
future together.

It suited our short-term purpose –
we never
intended to stay here
would not invest
too much in what's condemned.

Yet sometimes, shaken,
I try to picture
this place as salvage
after we leave, its parts
reverting to their source.
I try but can't, any more
than my own bones can feel
their sure conclusion – the sole
truth conceivable
being here, being now.

ANNIVERSARY

The year turned over
like soil –
roots   stumps   rubble
he meant to dispose of
given an airing
clearing the way for a new
calendar

She carries in the yield
I'd envy this
profusion
amid order –
something I've no success at

but who can measure it
so dependent
on givens –
how hard
the ground   how keen
the sun or shade   the knowledge
you begin with

She picks
her way across this plot
distinguishing the good
from the unwanted
as I never could

The day is ending
They finish digging

I'm waiting quiet as weeds around
the border

CUTS

1

You come nursing wounds scored in the line
of emotional duty,
wearing a public face so that I ask
nothing

but provide
R&R

co-opted before
I can protest
(by birthright
on her side)

but you don't want me
to approve or
engage in
recriminations

only to wait while you
get your bearings & head
back.

2

You draw me out like a
poultice –

I spread   in words

then you retreat
again to her   to your
own arena

I could fight too
have a good aim with
names.

Draw up the terms
treaty
or declaration –

There is nothing between
these.

3

Your son   my daughter
romp & spar
unmeaning parody
of our respective battles

this
civilian talk
ripped
to ribbons by their
crossfire

so we
project across them.

We never touch
We hardly meet
before
you must
be going.

Their small goodbye
kiss   cuts
me like a
remark.

Reconnaissance

All day we circle with banalities
certain the other is there
somewhere

you have the advantage
knowing
the terrain

Too much you say
I must cast off
impedimenta
things I thought
I needed

At night you near
me   lights out
I never know when
you'll strike

Desert
I cry
You look tempted
but say
Surrender
the metaphor

Why should I trust you
behind you I hear
the drums of men
encamped

I stand
naked
await your squad of
words
caresses
any of which might
kill

SPLIT
for my daughter

She is
discovering
the other
half of her
world   so newly
ripped into
by tremors
beyond her;
or call it
continental drift
natural   inevitable
there is no scale
for these
repercussions

no history to redeem
her dislocation –

she will draw her own
maps accordingly

& you & I
can only
watch with the small
dignity   of two
opposing shores
beaten on by the same
sea.

Things Like This

Nothing could dissolve here –
the scene is fixed like
those old photos
my grandmother doctored
truer than life

the jp & his wife have
time for their house now –
she maintains
the inside
like the room of
a dead loved one
purer than it ever was

he keeps up
the outside
the place smells suffocatingly of roses
each lawnblade lacquered & preserved
each flower nameless but
knowing its place
as they do now

The jp & his wife ask
no awkward questions but
witness as needed
our dissolution

their monstrous politeness
unpicks us like sutures
our weaknesses drip
all over their berber
they do not notice
used to things like this.

DECREE NISI

For a while I was
a novelty
dumb as a
pet

fully prepared
to learn
your ways
assimilate

my alien nature
almost currency.

When this wore off you
feared claims on
your territory.

It's true
I entered where
your shores were
unpatrolled,
made inroads on
your language –

I am
everywhere   there is
no being
rid of me.

Invader
you say
and at once I am
detained;

ask for
an interpreter
no one here
speaks
like me.

I camp on the
borders of
your life;

await
who knows
what fate:

I cannot
go home.

TEA FOR TWO

Scrambling eggs
for baby Kate –
curds rise from the milk like
the beginnings of an idea
remember
me

thirteen
frantically beating & scraping
for my Home Economics teacher
willing the viscous mess to jell
with some semblance of domestic
skill that would
certify me genuine
Golden Wattle
material.

I failed her class:
my stitching yielded
as soon as worn
my roasts after hours
stayed stubbornly red;
I could not please.

Yet nowadays these things
come easily
or those that don't
have sorted themselves out:
we don't eat meat, wear
off-the-rack
and no one's there
to watch
the clock.

BREAD

You always liked it, it was
my one success:

the sticky flesh
took life under
my hands,
swelled like
lungs

breathed
warm perfume through our
winter kitchen

Fast as I worked I could never
make it
outlast our
devouring

stomachs heavy as
lust but
summer came on, the delicate
balance needed for yeast
upset with the
heat

                Instead
my belly rose   my hands
grew full of preparations

No time then to knead
but only to wipe, soothe,
stroke to sleep our
little playdough features
as you called her

Now I buy bread others
have laboured over
she won't miss
what she never tasted

If anyone asks I'll say
I used to bake but
somewhere along the way I
lost the knack

You'd find the cupboard all but
bare
if you came back
if you came back.

PIANOFORTE

My baby tries the keys
in ways their maker
never meant.

At her age I longed
to run a loud hand
across the board
of Nana Bell's
piano.

Nana grew shrill
could not say why
she forbade it;
still rued the day she'd let
my brothers prod & thump
to their heart's content;
thought I should know better.

It puts the notes out   my mother
would plead
but I never could hear the difference.
Piano means softly   she always said.

Now, inherited, it's never played
except when Kate grunts
to be lifted – breaks open chords
with her fat fists.

She'll learn
in time
but not from me.

EVER AFTER

Let the grass cover
the attempt we made here
at cultivation

these rows you
abandoned
thrive like
Sleeping Beauty's gorse.

In the house lies a woman
crying
not sleeping.

The bedroom door hangs
on one hinge
the mirror is
shattered.

She'll always lie here
like this
always –
no kiss
will move her.

Again & again
I come back
to inspect
the exterior
looking for clues

to how we got here –
pull weeds
man-high & beyond my
strength   see

nasturtiums spreading to flower
yellow as bruises
the grass
taking over.

The Snow Queen

1

It was the view we shared
looking onto the street from the same
window – that began it.

Now I wander alone
wait for the sky to stop
dropping in shards
at my feet.

My body
bit by bit
feels
little but I can't
admit the winter   must

keep moving or the tears
congeal on my cheeks
as I gaze in
on the children   unwrapping.

Like one who froze
to death spending
her last matchlight
I dream –

It was the vision we shared.

2

He saw from the beginning it was ugly

Hitched his sled out of town
threw in his lot with a cold
heart & an eye
for my distances

What makes you think you can follow
& bring him back

He saw from the beginning it was ugly
You want everything to end
like fairytales

3

He has left me: I recall
suddenly, seasons outside
this witch's garden
where it seems a permanent summer
seeped into my bones & drained me
of all desire.

Now I am seized with a need
for snow   for a world
spinning off under my feet
                    What
was my name before
this spell

Quick   out
through the gate where roses caught
my eye   spots of blood
& I remembered

my own quest   not
as I thought for him

but out on the wind like the cruel
robber girl.

4 CROW

His tame sweetheart is a widow now
They grew old together
Black parody of your
ambitions.

Why does she not fly

She wears her crepe like a
leg-iron.

Post-Partum

1 Tracks

Silver as minnows, then pink
depending on light
they dart
from armpit to nipple
from hip to Mount
of Venus

Guidelines across
this body   a journey
my child has taken

hinting at loss
of limits

Once-invisible ink revealed
under heat

Secrets no one can take from us.

2 My Breasts

Will not be twelve years old again
for anyone   can't feign
uselessness

have little sense of humour   tend
to gravity   going their own way

A shape he says *only a
baby could love*

but I might too if not
for him   who says

Too wayward
who wants instead
'little pale strawberries'
and cream

who demands
that they stand to attention

My breasts ignore him, too bad,
I am learning from them.

DEADLOCK

1

My mother seemed
happy with her lot   stitching
pretty pictures in a high tower
but the blood fell and she remembered
suddenly the idea of me
I brought death like an appointment
she left me this other
who is after my heart   I run
for the dark wood   she will make do
with substitutes
thinking herself
rid of me

2

Never open the door to strangers
with your own face on
        hair as black as
        lips as red as
this is no mirror that is the sky I see
my world a glass box   I am
fixed in primary colours   stopped
as snow   unshiftable
as blood on your hands   ebony
to touch

3

One of us had to go and she
won out   her beauty
fits like a second skin
the only beauty permitted
in this kingdom

Each day she calls it up and I
look back at her
still   we can't escape
this deadlock   nothing
will make me
reach for that sky   or retch
the apple from my throat
the thing is lodged
for good.

& IF YOU SAID JUMP
IN THE RIVER I WOULD

Sinéad O'Connor

You want to fill
your pockets with me like
lead   the dead
weight you need
to stay down   I

curl into the smell
of you the overcoat of
miraculous sell
psst do you want

flashing your nothings
you want to fill
with me like gold

& I will burn
a hole with my
impatience to be
spent

& you will run
through years of me
in a week

IMPRINT

1

Leave like these bruises
that meet on each thigh
glossing the speech
of bodies

Here a smear
like chrism on throat

here on hip a note to the effect that
two lay side by side & looked
up away from bones colliding
through flesh & finding it
harder than thought

2

Caught caught your
wakefulness like a
tune to improvise on

interrogating the
order of things

By night there is no
object constancy

By night there are snakes
not in the head but
under the bed we
can't step out of

Rising as if to music

This gift sung back to you

3

First cigarettes measure this time
apart

Hot tips peel back toward fingers
too quickly

forge firebreaks through
the body   play
with damage like
language   a new
shade of rouge
a matter of bruises
something to butt out neatly

though already
each alveolus darkly
takes the imprint

though mouth's tang will always
be yours & fingers tarred
for good

NINE SOUTH

Man-mountain, invading
Gulliver
who came & went at
will

you lie here now
proven human
& I
so small
at liberty

uncomfortable with this
power, must

stay an
hour at least   to be
decent –

bring no meat   no wine
to soften my
advantage

only speak
in a language
you never attempted
to learn.

You gulp for air as
the nurse enters.

This is my daughter
you say
& I
grip
your hand   weak
as clay
sweat like
slip between
our palms

You won't
let go.

MERNA

Forgive me but I always pictured
Bertha of Thornfield or
a muppet-like creature
sweeping down corridors

when Dad said
you were
never seen
again

in chains
bucketed down to clean –

so Gothic.
Did he defend
your honour as he said or
just stand by
without a murmur
while you were beaten
into it

Merna,
they say
you were the brightest of
the lot
that you wrote poems
that you & I look
alike

Mum says
you are still
violent
but I don't
know what that
can mean
for a woman
in your position:

I will never
know I will
never know
how you
got there

Faye says she brought
you sweets & you were glad but
indifferent
to visitors

How then can I speak
to you   I must be
talking to
myself

PSYCH WARD

1 FLOWERS

They form a screen:
still life
around the narrow bed.

Daily you pluck out heads
as each one nods to signal
parting or
embarrassment.

Little markers
of how you got here
they drop off like friends.

The slimy stems
rot where they were cut
the stench
prevents sleep & yet
you don't
toss them out.

2 WAKE

At night the torch passes
divining sleep –

who's touched
by that unprescribable
angel
stirring the dead
waters.

You thought
oblivion would be better
like sleep but bigger:
a king wave.

Instead you were dumped
here   and now, by day,
we expect you to talk
with a mouth full of grit
a splitting head and
by night
to recede
open or shut, like a shell.

A VISITATION
for Julie

Pearse strides, three years old
through the stream
turned on at weekends
in this hospital garden.

Red mud, the stench of bores
clings to his buttocks.
Hiding naked in pampas grass
he steps out unscratched

traces the flow
to its end in a still lake
where ducks with young
scribble and punch out
their hunt for sustenance;

you, beside me on the bench
fuller than water
wipe him clean
restoring order

sketching futures on this
air dry as parchment
talk of a daughter
here
in your ninth month.

O.T.

1 WOOD

It won't quite work, it follows
someone else's template;
you trace around & force it
through the band-saw.

Some gift for a daughter:
this flightless bird
designed for amusement
clacking along.

Somebody else's room: the blades
teeth   drills you ease between
remembered from schooldays
yet unfamiliar.

The men make tables,
toolboxes.
They hum & whistle.

You clean up glue, sweep
shavings, wipe
hands on apron – spread
red paint that sticks like
blood on Bluebeard's
key.

2 CLAY

It is colder & warmer than flesh & there is
no centre to get at   no
end to it   there is always
more   infinitely
connectable

it moves even
under your feet
like a fluid

collects
impurities
which must be wedged
out or worked with –
every flaw a potential
feature.

There is no plan to follow here, only
what the mass itself suggests,
you read it
like an ink blot
the eyes of a
dreamer at lights
out   sensing the pulse.

Ready to feel
your way in
blurring the edges of
earth & water   it fits
second skin
takes your fingerprints
& forgets them

Pick a tool   peel back
the accidentals
surgeon or
murderer as
you choose.

PHONE

The voices are not
here in our head
but out in the real
world.

They call.
They decide
when we will leave
how we will go.

They say they tried
earlier but
couldn't get through.

This is the ward's hot-spot
this is where words crowd out
force connections.

This is where we learn
each other's names.